My Mom Is My SHOW-AND-TELL

Written and Illustrated by DOLORES JOHNSON

SCHOLASTIC INC.
New York Toronto London Auckland Sydney
Mexico City New Delhi Hong Kong

CAREER DAY

MARLA and MRS. LEE

ROBERT and MR. PEREZ

ISBN 0-439-18799-0

Published by Scholastic Inc., 555 Broadway, New York, NY 10012, by arrangement with Marshall Cavendish. SCHOLASTIC and associated logos are trademarks and/or registered trademarks of Scholastic Inc.

12 11 10 9 8 7 6 5 4 3 2 1   0 1 2 3 4 5/0

Printed in the U.S.A.   08
First Scholastic printing, September 2000

The text of this book is set in 14 point Slimbach Book.
The illustrations are rendered in watercolor.

SHOW & TELL

ERIN and DR. ABBOTT

To my art director,
Jean Krulis

My mom is coming to speak to my class today. My mom will be my show-and-tell. She has never ever talked to my class before. I don't know if she can handle it.

At breakfast I ask her, "Is that what you're wearing? If you want to change, I can pick out something. If this is too much for you, we can just call it off." But instead of taking me up on my offer, she gives me one of her funny looks.

I walk with her and talk to her on the way to school. What kind of son would I be if I didn't pass on what I know? "Don't tell any of your long stories. Talk up real loud, but don't shout. And whatever happens, under no circumstance, don't you dare call me Pumpkin."

All my mom says is, "I'll try to do my best . . . Pumpkin."

I give her one of my funny looks.

We have to cross the street. I make sure to look both ways. I grab her hand, and when no car is coming, we cross. I drop my mom's hand when we get to the other side. Someone I know might see me. But then another question comes up. "You're not going to hold my hand in front of all the other kids, are you, Mom?"

"No. But I do plan to give you six big, wet, sloppy kisses the very minute that I'm done."

"That reminds me, Mom. There'll be no spitting on tissues to clean my face. No tucking my shirt in my pants. Don't talk about when I was a little kid. And don't tell any of your silly jokes."

Mom laughs. "Not even the one about the penguin and the giraffe who meet at the supermarket?"

"Aw, Mom! Your jokes can be so corny."

But my mom isn't listening to me anymore. She is waving at Mrs. Thomas, who is sitting on her porch. Mrs. Thomas has been sitting in that same spot since the sky has been blue and the earth has been dirty.

"I'm counting on you, Mom. Don't show my baby book. Don't show that weird little curl of my hair that you saved. And don't you dare show any of my baby pictures, like you keep showing to Mrs. Thomas."

But of course my mom isn't listening to me. She is saying, "Mrs. Thomas. Would you like to see some more baby pictures? I've got a shot in my purse of my sweet little pumpkin here. He's so cute, you just want to hug him to pieces."

"Mom!" I yell. "Your purse looks so heavy. You'd better let me carry it for you." I carry her purse until we get past Mrs. Thomas's house. But then I give it back real quick before someone thinks it's mine.

"Mom, when you talk at show-and-tell, don't talk about the weird stuff you do at work. When Erin's mother, the doctor, came to my class, all she could talk about was bones and germs and bacteria. After she left, we all pretended that Erin was a bag of bones full of cooties!"

"Did everyone pretend or was it just you?"

"I wasn't the only one!" I sigh.

"Robert's father is a lawyer. He talked too much. He talked about nothing. It seemed he would never stop talking. All the kids were bored. Some kids fell asleep. One even started to snore."

"I heard," says my mother. "Your teacher told me that maybe you should be trying to get to bed a bit earlier."

"Can't a guy have a little fun?" I ask. "But, whatever you do, don't sing songs to us like Marla's mother did. Marla's mom thinks she's a great singer. But I'll tell you the truth. The rest of the kids think she's just kind of strange."

My mom says, "I've never even heard her sing, but somehow I know that Marla's mother is a great singer. That's because she loves to sing and she's not ashamed to show it. What good is a song you carry in your heart . . . if you can't let the whole world hear it?"

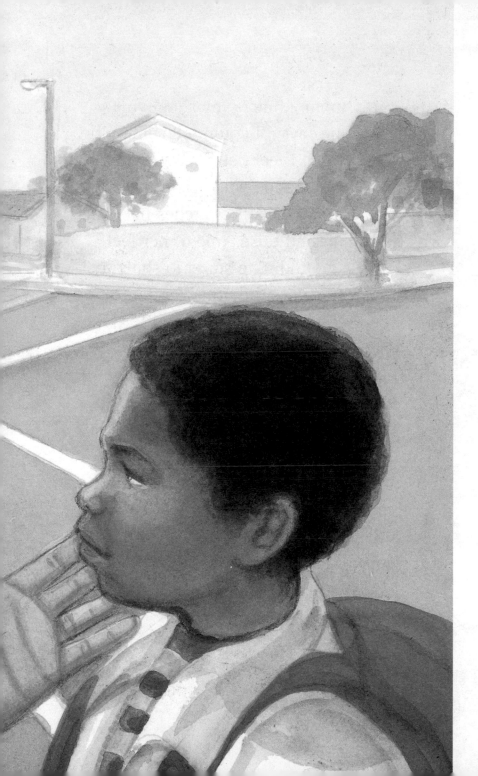

I stop in the middle of the sidewalk. "Oh no!" I say. "Is that what you are going to talk about, Mom? Are you going to spend the whole time talking to my class about that crazy kind of stuff? The rest of the guys will never let me hear the end of it."

"No, Pumpkin. I'm just going to talk about my job." She stops and turns around. The smile she's worn all morning is missing. "Isn't that what I'm supposed to be doing?" She lifts my chin and looks me right in the eye. "Will you still love me no matter what happens?"

I look down at the ground. "Your shoe's untied," I tell my mother. "I better tie it. You don't want to trip, do you?"

My mom admires my shoe-tying. Then she says, "I could tell something was wrong. I feel better now. When you tied my shoe you gave me—magic feet!" And my mother arches her arms in the air and raises one of her feet off the ground. She starts to shake her foot. She raises the other foot and then twists her hips back and forth right there on the sidewalk. Before I can stop her, she shuffles down the street, making a thousand funny little dance steps. I look around to see if anyone sees her. My face is heating up. My throat is getting tight. I try to call to her under my breath. "Mom, don't do that. Mom, please!" But she gets too far ahead.

My mother is close to the school by now. Up ahead, I can see kids who know me. Both Erin and Robert are at the front door watching my mom dance down the street. They start to laugh. Then they see me, and they must have remembered that it is Parent Show-and-Tell Day. That is when they really start to laugh. My mom, who dances by them, runs up the steps to the school building. Then she turns around to look for me. "Come on, Pum—David. We're going to be late."

I can't take another step. My feet have become part of the gray concrete. But then I hear a voice from behind me. "What fun, David. Your mom can really dance!" I turn around to see Marla, the singer's daughter. She is smiling at my mother. I don't say anything. I just run inside the building.

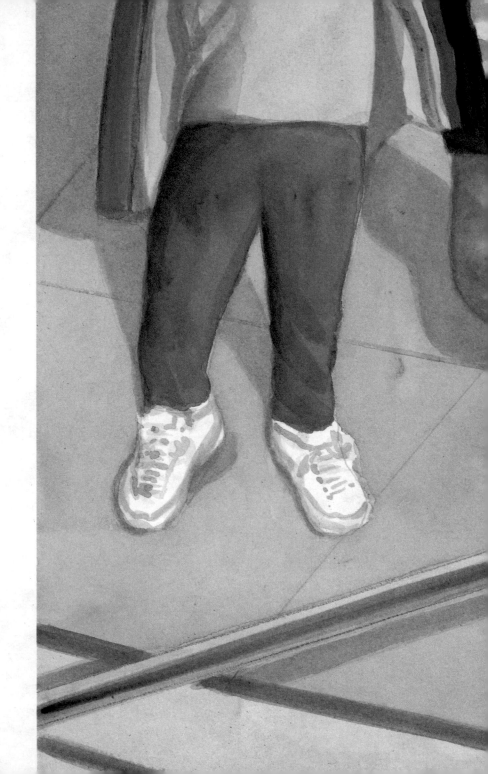

In the classroom, my teacher, Mrs. Adams, stands in the front of the room. "Today is a very important day, class. We have a visitor here to tell us about her job. It's David's mother, Mrs. Allie Spencer. David, would you introduce your mother, please?"

I get up slowly from my chair and stand in front of the room. I swallow real loud. I swallow again. "Would you like to hear the one about the penguin and the giraffe who meet in the supermarket?" The kids all laugh and say, "Yeah!"

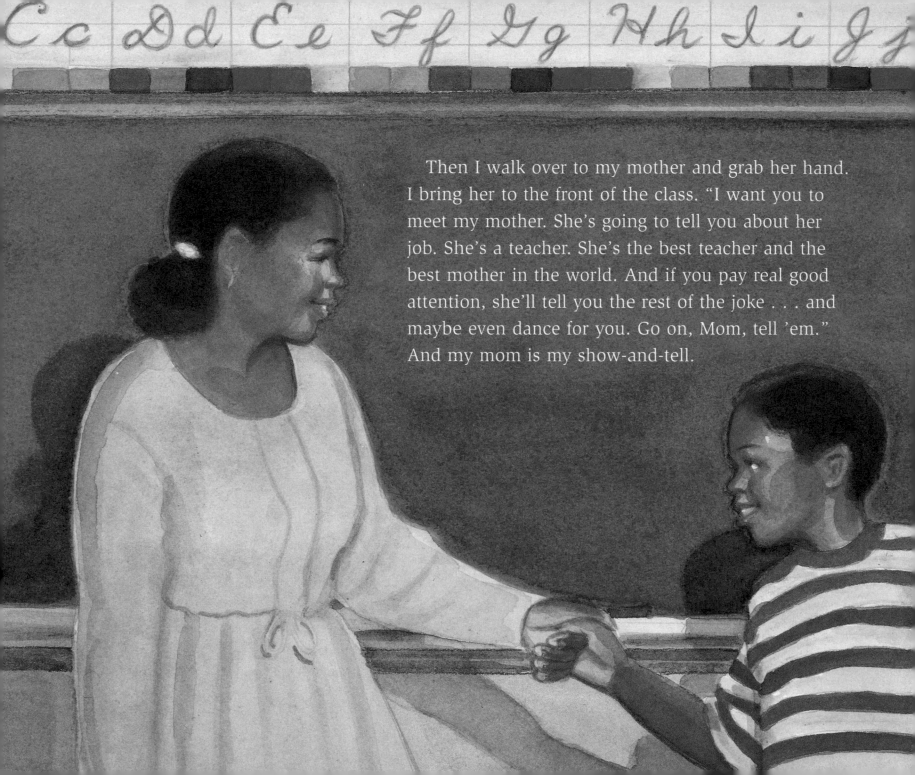

Then I walk over to my mother and grab her hand. I bring her to the front of the class. "I want you to meet my mother. She's going to tell you about her job. She's a teacher. She's the best teacher and the best mother in the world. And if you pay real good attention, she'll tell you the rest of the joke . . . and maybe even dance for you. Go on, Mom, tell 'em." And my mom is my show-and-tell.